**Also by John Leslie**

Blood on the Keys
Bounty Hunter Blues
Killer in Paradise
Damaged Goods
Havana Hustle

*Gideon Lowry Mysteries:*

Killing Me Softly
Night and Day

# LOVE FOR SALE